SNIPPY AND SNAPPY.

Other Books by Wanda Gág

———————————

Millions of Cats
The Funny Thing
Gone Is Gone
The ABC Bunny
Snow White and the Seven Dwarfs
Nothing at All

SNIPPY AND SNAPPY

BY WANDA GÁG

University of Minnesota Press
Minneapolis • London

The Fesler-Lampert Minnesota Heritage Book Series

This series is published with the generous assistance of the John K. and Elsie Lampert Fesler Fund and David R. and Elizabeth P. Fesler. Its mission is to republish significant out-of-print books that contribute to Minnesota's cultural legacy and to our understanding and appreciation of the Upper Midwest.

Published by the University of Minnesota Press
111 Third Avenue South, Suite 290
Minneapolis, MN 55401-2520
http://www.upress.umn.edu

Printed in the United States of America on acid-free paper

The University of Minnesota is an equal-opportunity educator and employer.

27 26 25 24 23 22 21   10 9 8 7 6 5 4 3

SNIPPY AND SNAPPY

Snippy and Snappy were two little field-mice.
Snippy was Snappy's sister.
Snappy was Snippy's brother.
They lived with their father and mother in
a cozy nook in a hay field.

They lived in a hay field,
A big grassy hay field,
A field full of flowers and fun.

Snippy and Snappy liked this big grassy
hay field and played in it all day long.

But when evening came, they hurried home to their cozy little nook, for then the light was lit and Mother Mouse sat and knitted jackets for her little family.

Father Mouse sat there too and read aloud from his newspaper. This newspaper was small enough for a mouse to read, and it was called THE MOUSE PAPER.

Father Mouse read about the big wide
world and the many big things in it.

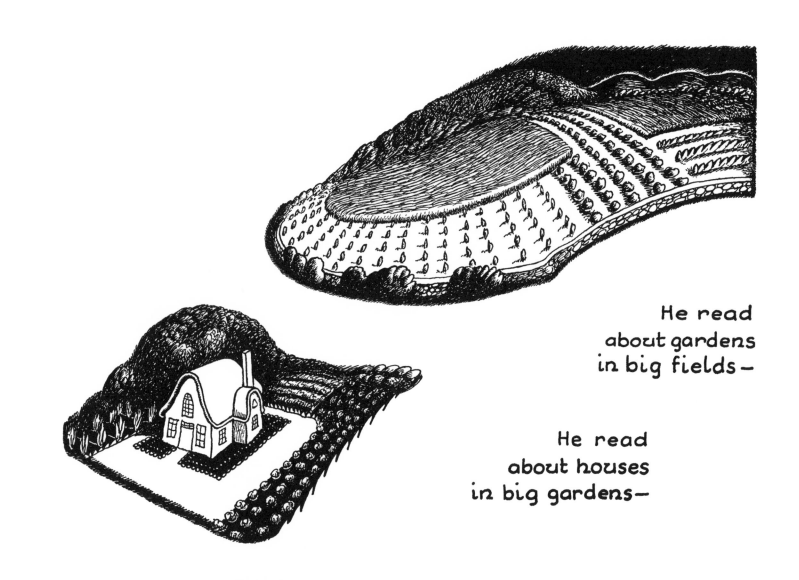

He read
about gardens
in big fields —

He read
about houses
in big gardens —

He read
about kitchen
cupboards in big houses—

But most often he read
about big yellow cheeses
in big kitchen cupboards!

"What is a kitchen cupboard?"
said Snippy to Snappy.
"Something with cheese in it,"
said Snappy to Snippy.
"I wish we could find a kitchen
cupboard full of cheese," said
Snippy, "for I'm very FOND of cheese."
"I too," said Snappy "I'm VERY
fond of cheese."

Now one day, as Snippy and Snappy were
playing with Mother Mouse's big blue knitting
ball, it rolled way outside of their cozy nook.

"Oh, let's roll it some more!" cried Snippy. "Maybe it will lead us somewhere."

"Oh yes," cried Snappy, "maybe it will lead us to a kitchen cupboard full of cheese!"

So they rolled it and rolled it.

They rolled it up, they rolled it down,
They rolled it up and up and down.
They rolled it up and DOWN and down,
They rolled it UP AND DOWN.

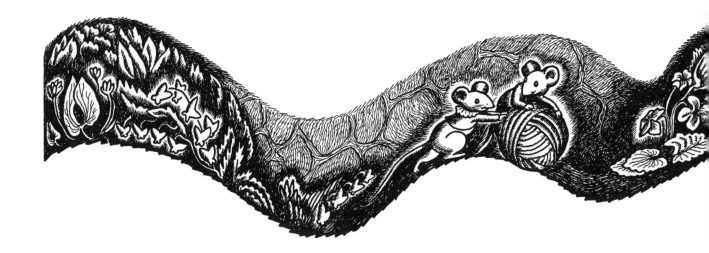

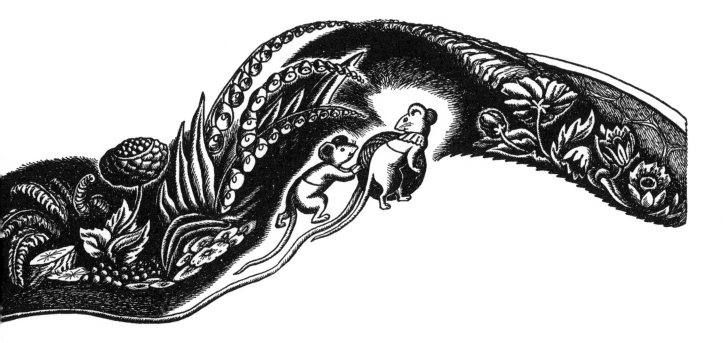

They rolled it over this and that,
And over things both round and flat,
And over things both small and tall,
Along a long, long garden wall.

But by and by they stopped.

"Let's sit down and rest awhile," said Snippy to Snappy. "I'm so hot and tired."

"Oh yes, let's," said Snappy to Snippy. "I'm so hot and tired too."

So they cuddled down under a tent of wild flowers and soon they were fast asleep.

But suddenly there was a
    rustle RUSTLE RUSTLE
and a bustle BUSTLE BUSTLE,
and before Snippy and Snappy knew what
had happened, something pink and plump
darted down among the flowers and snatched
up the big blue knitting ball.

Snippy jumped up and Snappy jumped up. They both grabbed the string of the knitting ball, and pulled at it. But the string broke in two, and Snippy and Snappy fell in a heap on the ground!

"We simply must get back that knitting ball," said Snippy.

"We simply must," said Snappy. "We'd better follow it!"

So they followed it.

They followed it up, they followed it down—They followed it up and up and down.

They followed it up and DOWN and down—They followed it UP AND DOWN.

They followed it over this and that, and over things both round and flat—

And over things both small and tall — AND THEN — ?

– over
the
garden
wall !

And what did Snippy and
Snappy see there?

"A house!" cried Snippy.

"Yes, a house!" cried Snappy.

"In houses there are kitchen
cupboards," said Snippy.

"And in kitchen cupboards
there is CHEESE," said Snappy.

Snippy and Snappy were so
excited about the cheese, they
forgot all about Mother Mouse's
big blue knitting ball.

They ran down the long path to the house and scampered in through the big open door.

But alas! poor Snippy, and alas! poor Snappy— there was no cheese to be seen. What they did see, though, made them open their eyes in wonder. How puzzled they were! You see, Snippy and Snappy were field-mice and had never been in a house before, so what could they know about all the things people have in their homes?

On the floor was a fuzzy rug with a border of flowers around it.

"What's this?" asked Snippy.

"It's a hay field, I guess," said Snappy, "only these flowers don't smell like flowers, and they're so flat we could never hide under them."

Then Snappy found a footstool which
had a green fringe around it.
"Look, Snippy," he cried, "here's a tree with
funny leaves, and it's a tree with FOUR trunks."

But Snippy had found a mop.

"Such a queer plant," she cried. "It has a wooden stem and not a SINGLE leaf — and its roots grow outside of the ground."

"Oh, that's nothing," said Snappy who was looking up at a standing lamp. "I've found a plant with its roots outside of the ground too— beautiful cur-r-r-ly roots. And MY plant has leaves and a flower besides— the BIGGEST flower I EVER saw!"

But Snippy did not hear. She had wandered into a long hall which had a mirror at the end of it.

"Oh, Snappy!" called Snippy.

"What is it, Snippy?" called Snappy.

"Come quick!" cried Snippy. "There's another mouse here—a little girl-mouse — and everything I do, she does too."

Snappy rushed out into the long hall and now, of course, there were two little mice in the mirror.

"Let's fight 'em!" cried Snappy, and he made a dash toward the mirror. But the boy-mouse in the mirror seemed to rush at them so FIERCELY that Snippy and Snappy turned around and scurried away as fast as they could.

"I don't like those copy-cat mice at ALL,"
said Snappy. "Let's hurry back home." So—

They darted here and darted there.
From fuzzy rug to fringy chair;
And ran with all their mousie-might
From floppy mop to flowery light.

But alas! poor Snippy, and alas! poor
Snappy. They couldn't find their way
out. The big door was closed now, and
it was getting dark too. The two field-
mice felt lost and little and lonely,
and soon they were crying as

though their hearts would break.

"Snuffle, Snuffle," went Snippy.

"Sniffle, Sniffle," went Snappy.

But suddenly Snappy perked up his nose. He stopped his, "Sniffle, Sniffle," and gave a "Sniff!
Sniff!
Sniff!" instead.

"What's up?" said Snippy. "Are you going to sneeze?"

"Oh no!" said Snappy. "I smell some CHEESE!"

Now, when a mouse smells cheese, he can find his way to it, even though the doors are closed. So before they knew it, Snippy and Snappy found themselves going through a crack in the wall and ——

"There it is!" cried Snappy, looking hungrily at a big chunk of cheese in —— A MOUSE TRAP!

He was just about to start nibbling at it, when Snippy gave a loud squeak.

"Oh, oh!" she cried. "Something's after us."
It was true. Something jumped down from
somewhere and ran after the two little field-mice.

"Snippy! Snappy! Don't you know me?" said a voice behind them. The two little mice looked around and whom should they see but Father Mouse! Snippy and Snappy pointed to the mouse-trap and said proudly, "See, Father Mouse? A kitchen cupboard full of cheese. We found it all by ourselves." But Father Mouse put his arms around Snippy and Snappy and said, "My dear little mice—that is NOT a kitchen cupboard— it's a MOUSE TRAP."

"And what's a mouse-trap?" asked Snippy and Snappy.

"Well," said Father Mouse, "as soon as a mouse starts nibbling at the cheese in a mouse-trap —
there's a snip and a snap
and a trip and a trap —
and that's the end of a little mousie."
"Oh dear, oh dear," said Snippy and Snappy.
Now Father Mouse went to a corner and came back with two big chunks of cheese. He put one under each arm, and off he went —
Zip! Zip! thru a crack in the wall. And
Zip! Zip!
Zip! Zip! went Snippy and Snappy after him.

Outdoors the moon was shining brightly, and when they reached their cozy little nook Mother Mouse was waiting for them.

"Where have you all been so long?" asked Mother Mouse, "I've been so lonely—and quite lost without my knitting ball, for I can't find it anywhere."

Snippy looked at Snappy.

Snappy looked at Snippy, and they both burst into tears.

"Never mind if it's lost," said Mother Mouse. "I won't scold you—but do tell me all about it."

"Well," said Snippy, "We rolled it and rolled it."
"Yes," said Snappy,
    "We rolled it up, we rolled it down,
    We rolled it up and up and down.
    We rolled it up and DOWN and down,
    We rolled it UP AND DOWN."

"And then a pink plump thing came and snatched it from us, and we followed it," said Snippy.

"Yes," said Snappy,

"We followed it over this and that,
And over things both round and flat,
And over things both small and tall,
And then! — over the garden wall."

"Where there was a house," said Snippy,

"All full of flat flowers
And the funniest trees,
With copy-cat mice
And a trap full of cheese!"

"A trap full of cheese!" cried Mother Mouse.
"Yes," laughed Father Mouse, "but you know
where there's cheese, why there am I, so—"
"So, of course he saved us," said Snippy.
"Yes, of course he did," said Snappy.

"And," said Snippy and Snappy,
"We'll NEVER

NEVER

NEVER

NEVER

go near a house or a mouse trap again."

And Snippy and Snappy
NEVER

NEVER

NEVER

NEVER did,
so of course they didn't get caught
and lived happily ever, ever, ever after.

Wanda Gág (1893–1946) is best known for her Newbery Honor classics *Millions of Cats* and *ABC Bunny*. Born in New Ulm, Minnesota, the eldest daughter of Bohemian immigrants, she achieved international acclaim as a children's book author, artist, and illustrator. She was an inventive printmaker and an influential member of the vibrant New York art community during the 1920s and 1930s. Her books *The Funny Thing* and *Gone Is Gone, or the Story of a Man Who Wanted to Do Housework* are also available from the University of Minnesota Press.